TALES OF BONG TREE ISLAND

(Interviews with Descendants of The Owl and The Pussycat)

A Story for the Inner Child in Everyone

Written and Illustrated by E.J. Lefavour

TALES OF BONG TREE ISLAND

Signature Book Printing, Inc.
www.sbpbooks.com
Printed in the U.S.A.

ISBN 978-0-615-67402-5

Printed 2012
First Edition

Published by Khan Studio
Gloucester, MA
For more information visit:
www.khanstudiointernational.com

Illustrations, Cover and Back Design
by E.J. Lefavour

Contents

Dedication and Acknowledgements

This book is dedicated to all the good people of Cape Ann, fellow contributors and friends of Good Morning Gloucester, and especially to my dear friends, Wendie Demuth and Joey Ciaramitaro.

The book you are holding was made possible by the generous Kickstarter support of the following people who donated $50 or more toward the first printing of this book. There were others too numerous to list who pledged smaller amounts and were also instrumental in this book coming into being:

Lily & Stevie Bromberger, Peabody, MA from Mary Bowles
Eric Smith, Gloucester, MA
Marty and Barbara Luster, Gloucester, MA
Judith Monteferrante, Gloucester, MA
Chris Murray, Mexico
Claudia Orta, Mexico
For My Grandchildren, Catherine Wilson
Paul Morrison, Sue Lovett & Rubber Duck, Rockport, MA
Henry and Carolyn Landry Poughkeepsie, NY
Jim Flint, Lanesville, MA for Sylvan, age 5
Carol McKenna, Gloucester, MA
Bob and Ann Kennedy, Liberty, MO
Wendie Demuth, Gloucester, MA
Joan C. Quigley
Alma McLaughlin, Gloucester, MA
Rosemary Quarato, Gloucester, MA
Great Job! Dad and Kerstin, Dover, NH
Eloise and Madeline Ciaramitaro
Susan McKain, Gloucester, MA
Karen Ristuben, Gloucester, MA
Adriana "Gigi" Mederos, Swampscott, MA
In Memory of Melinda - Deborah Rocco
Brenda Malloy, Gloucester, MA
Dona Lambert, Rockport, MA

Acknowledgements Cont'd.

Kathy and Steve Archer, Beverly, MA
Jim Yancey and Judy Howard - Bong Tree Island's first BBQ
Tom O'Keefe, Rockport, MA
Dedicated to the big little sister who could – Judy Wilburn
and the big little brother, Blake Lefavour
Lindsay Crouse, Gloucester, MA
Joan Spadorcia
Jan Shields - To my Loved Ones
Deb Schradieck
Joseph Matta and Gaille Thompson-Matta
Meg Lee and Family
Jim Raycroft dedicated to granddaughter, Tessa Alden Raycroft
Diana Long, Gloucester, MA
Marcia DeFelice, Manchester, MA
Victoria Koertge, Holden, MA
Tom Dow, Retired Landmark School Teacher
Wayne Valzania
Homalyn Krakowski, NYC
Kirsti Jespersen
Lyn Cardinal, Mixed Media Collage Painter
EL JEFE: From PR-MHD-Salem-NYC-GLOSTA'
Michele Dickeson - Benjamin Witten, Tewksbury, MA
Evelyn Howe, Gloucester, MA
D+MH Landergren, Gloucester, MA
Katrina Parson
Penny Warren, In memory of our beloved Nugie
Jean Anscombe, Gloucester, MA
Gail Miller, East Boston, MA
Dahlia Lee Newman and Lily Brooks Gray, Gloucester, MA
Chase Ahearn, Gloucester, MA
Fr Matthew Green, in memory of Pamela Sadler of Dayville, CT
Deborah von Rosenvinge, Rockport, MA
James & Julia Sanfilippo, Gloucester, MA
Ed Collard, Gloucester, MA
Heidi and Scott Wood
Janice and John Wood, Vestal, NY

Introduction

The author of the poem *The Owl and The Pussycat*, published in 1871, was an Englishman named Edward Lear (1812 - 1888). In case you are not familiar with his poem, or have forgotten parts of it, the poem goes:

> *The Owl and the Pussycat went to sea*
> *In a beautiful pea-green boat,*
> *They took some honey, and plenty of money,*
> *Wrapped up in a five pound note.*
> *The Owl looked up to the stars above,*
> *And sang to a small guitar,*
> *"O lovely Pussy! O Pussy, my love,*
> *What a beautiful Pussy you are, you are, you are,*
> *What a beautiful Pussy you are."*
> *Pussy said to the Owl "You elegant fowl,*
> *How charmingly sweet you sing.*
> *O let us be married, too long we have tarried;*
> *But what shall we do for a ring?"*
> *They sailed away, for a year and a day,*
> *To the land where the Bong-tree grows,*
> *And there in a wood a Piggy-wig stood*
> *With a ring at the end of his nose, his nose,*
> *With a ring at the end of his nose.*
> *"Dear Pig, are you willing to sell for one shilling your ring?"*
> *Said the Piggy, "I will"*
> *So they took it away, and were married next day*
> *By the Turkey who lives on the hill.*
> *They dined on mince, and slices of quince,*
> *Which they ate with a runcible spoon.*
> *And hand in hand, on the edge of the sand.*
> *They danced by the light of the moon, the moon,*
> *They danced by the light of the moon.*

What Mr. Lear didn't tell us is that the owl and the pussycat (named Barney and Caterina) were the subject of interspecies relationship discrimination, forced to run away from home so that they could be together, and had many kindlebroods of owlittens, which grew up to be owlpusses - the descendants of *The Owl and The Pussycat*. Maybe he didn't know. Most people don't because owlpusses stay on Bong Tree Island and not many people know how to get there, so they are seldom seen.

He also didn't tell us where Barney and Caterina came from, how they met, where they got the pea green boat, or why they sailed away in the first place.

This book will tell you all that and much more. But first, a little about how this book came into being.

I was not thinking of writing about the owl and the pussycat, or writing at all for that matter. I was in painting mode, working on a series of abstract glass paintings. There was one painting I was not happy with and decided it needed to become something else. I kept looking at it, waiting for it to show me what it wanted to be. All I kept seeing was an owl, so an owl it became. I have always loved owls. I also love my cats.

I went on to paint a number of owl paintings. Then a poem from my childhood, *The Owl and The Pussycat*, popped into my head and wouldn't leave -- like an earworm, those songs that stick and repeat over and over again in your head for days that you can't get rid of, no matter how hard you try. So I went back to the owl paintings and turned them into owlpusses, at which point the story starting evolving to go along with the paintings. The more I painted, the more the story evolved, until I ended up with this.

An interesting thing occurred while I was working on the Tales of Bong Tree Island paintings. Each time I entered my studio to paint, a mourning dove would sit in the tree outside my window and coo. If you have ever heard a mourning dove, you know it sounds just like an owl, and is often confused for one. It goes: "hooOOoo, hooo, hooo".

Doves also symbolize higher love, peace, grace, promise, devotion, divinity, and hopefulness, all of which are aspects of this book and its characters. I believe that dove was my muse. My cats "Little Bit" and "Van Gogh" helped too.

I hope you enjoy reading *Tales of Bong Tree Island* as much as I enjoyed being involved in its creation.

E.J. Lefavour
Gloucester, MA
July, 2012

CHAPTER I

IN THE BEGINNING:
THE OWL AND THE PUSSYCAT

Farmer Bates' plants and livestock were well cared for and flourished. Each animal had a name, was loved like a pet and would follow Griffin and Penelope around the property. Since they had fresh fish, eggs and vegetables to eat, and sufficient money from the sale of Penelope's knitted goods and Griffin's tomatoes and flowers, they never sold or slaughtered any of their animals, who all lived happily until they died of old age.

In addition to their livestock, they also had an English sheepdog named Buster who kept track of the sheep, and a cat, named Millie, who lived in the barn and controlled the mouse population. There were also a pair of barn owls and a family of ferrets who lived in the barn, a family of hedgehogs who lived in the hedgerows around the property, and some bunnies who visited regularly and ate the clover in the yard, but never touched the vegetables or flowers. Hummingbirds, dragonflies and butterflies were also daily visitors to their beautiful gardens.

One spring morning in 1850, a double miracle of birth occurred at the Bates' farm. The brood of the resident barn owls, who coincidentally were also named Griffin and Penelope, began to hatch at the same time Millie the barn pussycat went into labor and began giving birth to her first kindle of kittens.

The first egg of Griffin and Penelope finally cracked open and out emerged the most beautiful little boy owlet. The parents smiled at each other, eyes gleaming, and Penelope said:
"Let us name him Barney, after your father." Griffin was very pleased and proud.

At that same moment, the first of Millie's kittens emerged. She was a beautiful pure white ball of fur, whose eyes, once they opened, would be a luminous tourquoise blue.

Millie beamed lovingly through her exhaustion of labor, and whispered to her baby girl: "Your name will be Caterina, which means pure."

Unfortunately, as is the case with many barn cats, the identity of Caterina's father was not known, so he did not get to share in the wonder of his very special daughter's birth.

"Barney and Caterina's First Encounter"

At around the age of 3 months, Barney and Caterina started moving away from their nest and litter in the barn to do some exploring and test out their newly discovered skills. Barney had just started learning to fly, and Caterina was out in the garden practicing her hunting skills and attempting to catch a mouse when they encountered each other for the first time. Of course, Barney had never seen a kitten before and Caterina had never met an owlet.

They immediately found each other fascinating and started asking each other many questions like:

"What is it like to fly? What is it like to have four legs? Why is your tail so long? Why don't you have feathers? How do you eat without a beak? How do you eat with a beak? What do you like to eat?"

Both liked mice, so they had food in common.

Barney and Caterina quickly became best friends, talking, playing, chasing each other around the barn and sharing mice.

Caterina's mom, Millie and Barney's parents, Griffin and Penelope, were good neighbors and friends (Griffin had even brought mice to Millie while she was nursing her kittens) and found their offspring's friendship and fascination with each other cute, but a little disconcerting. Neither seemed interested in playing or spending time with their siblings or others their own age and kind, preferring to spend most of their time together.

As the years passed and they reached their teens, Barney and Caterina's relationship started to change. They suddenly began seeing each other as opposite sexes, and their feelings toward each took on a new exciting and confusing dimension that neither could quite understand.

One day as they were hanging out together in the garden behind the barn, talking about subjects of a lofty nature, Barney suddenly leaned over and kissed Caterina. The earth moved, their hearts skipped a beat, and they both swooned a little.

Barney's father Griffin happened to be perched on the roof of the barn scanning the field for mice and glanced down just in time to see Barney and Caterina kissing. He immediately flew into the barn and called to his wife and Caterina's mother, Millie, and told them what he had witnessed.

The mothers became very alarmed. Millie exclaimed:
"This is not right -- owls and pussycats can certainly be friends, as we are, but that sort of behavior is strictly taboo."

They decided it was time to have a serious talk with their offspring before things got any more out of hand. Millie called Caterina, and Griffin and Penelope called Barney into the barn.

The parents told Barney and Caterina to sit down and then Griffin looked at Barney and said:

"I was on the roof of the barn just now and saw what looked like you and Caterina kissing. Now we understand that the teen years can be confusing as you are growing, becoming sexually mature and figuring out who you are, but you have to realize that while owls and pussycats can certainly be friends, they were never meant to be together that way."

Then Millie looked at Caterina and said:

"As your parents, we agree that it is time for you to start expanding your friendships to those of your own kind. You will have to start seeing less of each other."

17

Barney and Caterina were shocked and confused, and then became angry. Barney's feathers got ruffled and Caterina pinned her ears back. She glared at her mother and said:

"Our families have always been neighbors and friends, Barney and I grew up together and have been inseparable our whole lives, and now we are in love." She glanced at Barney to make sure he was in agreement with what she was saying. He smiled and nodded. Caterina continued:

"How can you all be so small-minded as to think there is something wrong with that, or that we shouldn't be together? What difference does it make that he is an owl and I a pussycat? We love each other, and nothing can change that."

At that point, their parents got upset and said:

"We are the adults, and while you two are still under our (or farmer Bates') roof, you will do as we say. You are still young and naive and do not understand the consequences of your actions. We can't even imagine what the neighbors would think and say if they found out."

Barney and Caterina both cried out in unison:
"What do we care what the neighbors think!? They have nothing to do with us!"

The parents angrily replied:
"Enough! This discussion is over. Go to your sleeping places."

To keep peace in the families, for a time Barney and Caterina cooled things and started spending time with some of the owls and pussycats their own age around Ramsgate. But try as they might not to, they always ended up running into each other, and the flame just burned brighter between them. They began arranging secret meetings away from the farm so they could be together.

One day as they were fooling around in the woods beyond the meadow, Barney stopped, looked adoringly at Caterina and started to croon:
"Oh my lovely Caterina, oh Caterina, my love, what a beautiful creature you are, you are, what a beautiful creature you are. Oh let us be married, too long we have tarried, let us run off and be married soon."

Caterina beamed and sang back to him:
"Oh Barney, my Barney, you elegant fowl, how charmingly sweet you sing. I would run off with you and marry today, with you I would do anything."

They both realized at that moment that they could no longer bear being apart, and started making plans to run away and get married.

Caterina thought it would be exciting to sail and since Barney walked too slowly and she couldn't fly, it seemed the perfect way for them to travel. Barney agreed and said that he knew of a beautiful little pea green boat for sale at Ramsgate Harbor that Osgood Bates had built, and would go the next day and talk to him about it.

The next day Barney visited Osgood Bates and explained their situation to him. Osgood was a true romantic and sympathized with their plight, so gave the beautiful pea green boat to Barney so that he and Caterina could sail away and be together.

They made their plans to leave on December 31st, so that they could end the old year and start the new together as a couple. No one would ever be able to tell them they couldn't be together again.

They departed Ramsgate Harbor at 6:00am on December 31, 1869, carrying nothing with them but some shillings wrapped in a five-pound note and a runcible spoon that Caterina had found in the barn (most likely filched from Mrs. Bates and hidden there by the ferrets). It was said that they also carried honey, but that is not true, as neither of them liked honey at all. They did however convince a sack full of mice to join them.

A year and a day later, on January 1, 1871, they landed on a beautiful island where bong trees grew, and immediately encountered hedgepiggywigs and hummingbunnybirds. They realized that interspecies marriage was totally accepted and embraced on the island, so they decided this would be the perfect place to make their new home and life together.

CHAPTER II

ABOUT MARTINE BATES

Martine Bates is an artist, genealogist and explorer who calls Gloucester, Massachusetts home. She has spent her life traveling the world, discovering and exploring little known tribes, cultures and creatures. Martine is best known for her discovery of the Itsybitsy Tribe of Southern Zolandia, with whom she lived for many years, as well as her study on the androgynous nature of the exceedingly tall and hairless Yuhuu Tribe in the mountainous regions of Yuhuululand.

The Itsybitsies are distantly related descendants of the Lilliputians who Lemuel Gulliver discovered in 1699. As a young girl, Martine was fascinated and greatly inspired by the stories of Lemuel Gulliver and his travels, and since childhood had aspired to become a great explorer like him.

Amongst her many other adventures, explorations and accomplishments, she is also an excellent photographer and sailor, and also enjoys painting, as well as writing.

Martine was born on Thanksgiving Day in 1974 to a seafaring family of fishermen and boat builders who came to Gloucester from England in 1856. Her great grandfather was Dutton Bates of Ramsgate, brother of Griffin Bates, who owned the farm where Barney and Caterina were born. Her grandfather was Charles Bates, Dutton's oldest son. Her father is Roger Bates, middle son of Charles Bates.

After Griffin and Penelope Bates died suddenly and mysteriously in their bed in 1853, Dutton and his sons and daughters-in-law moved to America. They chose Gloucester because of its world renown as a great and beautiful fishing and shipbuilding port. Dutton also had a lifelong friend, Captain Elias Davis, from County Hereford, England who had moved to Gloucester years earlier and wrote him often extolling its virtues and encouraging him to visit. As the sole beneficiary to Griffin and Penelope's estate, their sudden passing made it possible for all of them to go to America.

Martine grew up reading and enjoying The Owl and The Pussy-cat, and had always thought it would be exciting to locate and explore the land where the bong trees grow and learn more about Barney and Caterina, who had gotten their start at her great granduncle's farm.

Martine had done much research attempting to determine the location of Bong Tree Island. During her research, she came across an account of an explorer and photographer, named Alpheus Pomfry, who had sailed from England in 1908 in search of the land where the Bong Trees grow. He had never returned and was presumed lost at sea.

Eventually Martine was able to track down and make contact with a surviving relative of Mr. Pomfry, a great nephew named Pip Pomfry, who allowed her to go through a box of old papers and photographs in the attic that had belonged to his great uncle.

In the box, along with many wonderful old photos, letters and notes, Martine found a map that Mr. Pomfry had drawn of where he believed the land where the Bong Trees grow to be located. He believed it was an island, and referred to it as Bong Tree Island in his notes and on his map. Martine was considered by many to be an exceptional cartographer, and she hoped one day to be able to see how good Mr. Pomfry's cartographic skills had been.

Due in large part to her ancestry and connection to The Owl and The Pussycat, as well as her renown as an explorer, one day Martine was contacted by the Queen of England and invited to lead an expedition to locate Bong Tree Island. The Queen wished her to photograph and conduct interviews with some of the descendants of Barney and Caterina, and to see if she could find out what had happened to Mr. Pomfry, who had been a good friend of the Queen's mother.

The Queen offered to provide her with a seaworthy vessel and supplies to make the year and a day journey. Martine excitedly agreed on the condition that a full supply of paints, brushes and canvases be included in the supplies, so she could paint while on the journey. This turned out to be a very fortuitous request on her part.

Martine set sail on December 31, 2010 from Ramsgate Harbor, as The Owl and The Pussycat had done 161 years before. Her journey was filled with many adventures, mishaps and hair-raising events too numerous to describe in detail here, but included being pursued by pirates, and nearly run over by a cargo ship in a dense fog one night.

A year and a day later, on January 1, 2012, Martine landed on Crescent Moon Beach on Bong Tree Island. She knew she was in the right place when she saw the beautiful pea green boat on the shore, in surprisingly pristine condition, filled with flowers.

As Martine stepped onto the beach, she encountered an elegant and handsome creature, who greeted her and said: "Welcome. My name is Sir Winfred Owlpuss III. We seldom have visitors from the land beyond the line. Pray tell, what brings you here?"

Martine introduced herself and explained the reason for her visit. She then asked Sir Winfred if she could have permission to photograph, paint and interview him and some of the other descendants of Barney and Caterina, so that the Queen and people in the land beyond the line could get to know about them and Bong Tree Island.

Sir Winfred agreed to allow her paint and interview him, and said he would arrange interviews for her with some of the others, but that Martine would only be allowed to paint them because photographs were prohibited on Bong Tree Island. Upon hearing this she was so glad that she has requested the painting supplies from the Queen. It would have been horrible to come all this way with a camera only to find she couldn't use it, and not have art supplies with her to capture everything.

Sir Winfred went on to explain that a man by the name of Mr. Alpheus Pomfry had visited Bong Tree Island with a camera in 1909. The owlpusses and other inhabitants of Bong Tree Island at that time gave Mr. Pomfry permission to photograph them. He was said to be a pleasant man who stayed with them for a few full moons and took many photos.

He went on to recount the story passed down in Bong Tree history of the devastating storm, called "The Mr. Pomfry Storm".

It is told that shortly after Mr. Pomfry's departure, disaster struck Bong Tree Island. A storm like none of the owlpusses or other inhabitants had ever experienced before hit the island with a force of devastating winds and rain. Many of the owlpuss nests and eggs were destroyed, more than a dozen young owlittens drowned and many of the older owlpusses suffered broken wings while attempting to save the young and protect their families and themselves from the tempest.

When the storm had subsided, they looked out toward the line on the sea and saw Mr. Pomfry's boat capsized and sinking. He and his camera were never seen again.

At that moment, it was decided that Mr. Pomfry's camera and the photographs he had taken were the cause of the disaster and all vowed never to allow anyone to photograph them again.

Sir Winfred said that he personally did not believe that Mr. Pomfry caused the storm, but most on the island did and it was now part of their accepted history and beliefs.

Martine was sorry to hear about Mr. Pomfry's demise, but thrilled to have gotten one of the answers she was seeking within such a short time of arriving on Bong Tree Island.

Sir Winfred then offered to show her to a river surrounded by soft grasses and fruit trees where she could freshen up and rest, and said they would talk more later.

After Martine returned home she did some research and found that in 1909, there had been a large and deadly Category 3 hurricane, called the 1909 Grand Isle Hurricane, that had caused severe damage and killed hundreds of people in Cuba. She believes it was the effects of this hurricane, and not Mr. Pomfry, that caused the devastating storm that hit Bong Tree Island.

CHAPTER III

A LITTLE ABOUT
BONG TREE ISLAND

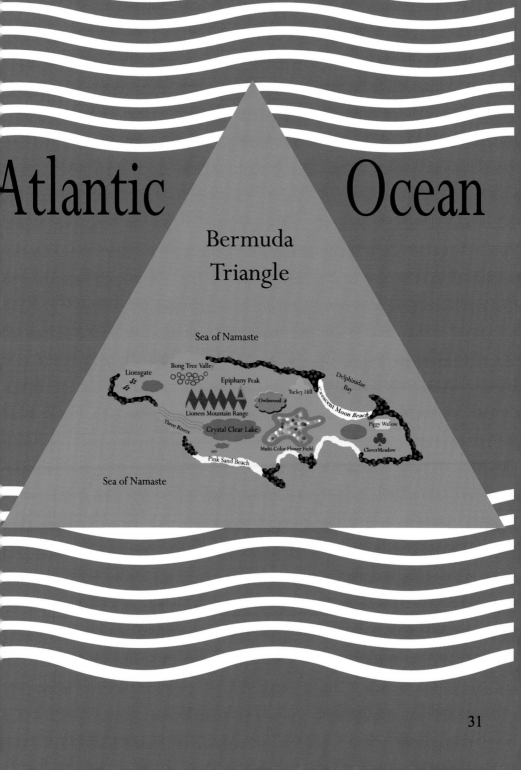

Atlantic Ocean

Bermuda Triangle

Sea of Namaste

Lionsgate
Bong Tree Valley
Epiphany Peak
Delphinidae Bay
Turkey Hill
Owlwood
Crescent Moon Beach
Lioness Mountain Range
Three Rivers
Crystal Clear Lake
Piggy Wallow
Multi-Color Flower Field
CloverMeadow
Pink Sand Beach

Sea of Namaste

Bong Tree Island is a magical place. It is a subtropical island located in the Atlantic Ocean in the middle of the Bermuda Triangle, in an uncharted sea called The Sea of Nemaste. The actual coordinates cannot be divulged, as it would be disastrous for the owlpusses and other inhabitants of Bong Tree Island if humans were to find it and start building resorts and malls. It is also extremely difficult to find, even if its coordinates were given. You have to enter the Bermuda Triangle to reach it, and that is a rather hit or miss thing to do; then there is no guarantee you will get back out again even if you do find your way in.

At about 155 miles long and 57 miles wide, Bong Tree Island is slightly larger than the Island of Jamaica, and has very similar topography. There are beautiful hills and mountains, lush tropical forests and woods, expansive fields filled with multi-colored flowers, crystal clear lakes, rivers, spring fed ponds, waterfalls, lovely white and pink sand beaches surrounded by a rocky coastline with cliffs and caves.

On the southeast coast is Crescent Moon Beach at Delphinidae Bay, a deepwater bay populated by dolphins, whales, playful sharks, colorful tropical fish and coral reefs. Martine was led to Bong Tree Island by a large pod of dolphins that she met up with upon entering the Bermuda Triangle.

Whenever you are at Crescent Moon Beach, you hear the constant chatter of the dolphins frolicking off the shore. If you go in the water and dunk your head under, you can hear a beautiful chorus of whale songs.

Just to the east of Crescent Moon Beach is Pigs Wallow, where the descendants of the pig who sold the ring to Barney and Caterina live. There is also a prickle of hedgepiggywigs that live nearby. Hedgepiggywigs are the offspring of hedgehogs and piggywigs, and are very charming creatures. As smart and friendly as we all know pigs are, hedgepiggywigs are even more clever and amiable.

These three hedgepiggywig friends are named Paul, Joey and Ed, and are known to be the smartest, most helpful and knowledgeable about the goings on around Bong Tree Island.

Hedgepiggywig Paul is a scientist and considered by many to be something of a genius. He studies the stars and planets, weather and microscopic changes in the atmosphere. Hedgepiggywig Paul does not agree with the Mr. Pomfry Storm theory, and calls it a crock of wiggypicklepoo. You always see Hedgepiggywig Paul with a rubber duck that he found washed up on the shore at Crescent Moon Beach in 1993, which he carries with him every where he goes.

Hedgepiggywig Joey is the friendliest and most outgoing, and the leader of the group. His larger ears allow him to hear everything that is going on around Bong Tree Island and report whatever might be of interest to anyone, sort of like the town crier. He thinks Hedgepiggywig Paul's rubber duck is silly.

Hedgepiggywig Ed is the most helpful and community minded of all the inhabitants of Bong Tree Island, and will stop whatever he is doing to help anyone in need of assistance with anything.

Most mornings you can find these three at the field of multi-colored flowers where they meet for breakfast.

"Hedgepiggywigs Paul, Joey and Ed"

To the west of Crescent Moon Beach is Turkey Hill, where the descendants of the turkey that married Barney and Caterina reside. The turkeys still officiate marriages on Bong Tree Island, but only on Weddingdays, which is our Wednesday.

The owlpusses have different names for the days of the week. For example:

• Monday is Moonday (when everyone dances by the light of the moon, except when there isn't one).

• Tuesday is Travelday (when everyone flies to a part of the island they haven't been to before, or that they particularly like visiting).

• Wednesday is Weddingday (the only day of the week that weddings are officiated on Bong Tree Island).

• Thursday is Nestday (when everyone cleans and repairs their nests).

• Friday is Frienday (when everyone does something fun with their friends).

• Saturday is Scatterday (when seeds are scattered so that new plants can grow).

• Sunday is Sandbathday, when everyone goes to the beach for a sand bath to keep their feathers fresh and shiny.

The climate on Bong Tree Island is perfect. The daytime temperature reaches a high of around 82 degrees, and at night it goes down to about sixty degrees. The sun rises at 6:00 every morning and sets at 8:30 every night. Every morning from 4:00-5:30 there is rain - a nice steady rain. The rest of the time it is sunny and clear with some unique cloud formations passing by to provide pieces of shade and wonderful shapes in the sky. The reason the climate is so ideal is because Bong Tree Island is located inside the Bermuda Triangle and bad weather normally can't find its way in.

Aside from owlpusses, the other inhabitants of the island include a clan of pigs (which symbolize abundance and happiness), the descendants of Oliver, the pig who sold his nose ring to Barney so that he and Caterina could wed. There is also a flock of turkeys (which symbolize abundance, awareness, generosity and nobility), who are direct descendants of Greer, the turkey on the hill who married The Owl and the Pussycat. The turkeys still officiate all marriages on Bong Tree Island to this day. There are many different types of birds (including the rare Jeweled Doctor Hummingbunnybird, a member of the hummingbunnybird family that exists only on Bong Tree Island), insects (although none bite or sting), mice, rabbits, raccoons, spider monkeys, panda bears, sheep, tiny deer, wild ponies, ferrets, ferrowls, manaturtles, hedgepiggywigs, and numerous other interspecies creatures on Bong Tree Island.

Martine was told that there is also a pride of peaceful lions that live at a place called Lionsgate on the other side of the island. They spend most of their time lying around with lambs and eating grass. She was not able to see them while she was there, as they were on an extended retreat in seclusion, silence and meditation focusing on love, world peace and unity. She did get to visit the mysterious Lionsgate, but more about that later.

The only dwellers on Bong Tree Island that Martine did not particularly care for were a band of wraithlike creatures called the Missings, who moved silently and in a very creepy way through Owlswood late at night, and across the moors at Lionsgate in the pre-dawn hours. Sir Winfred said they were the spirits of those lost in the Bermuda Triangle who have not yet accepted that they are dead, and are still searching for a way home. The missing are disembodied spirits, neither male nor female, young nor old, with mournful faces that reminded Martine of Edvard Munch's painting "The Scream". She encountered them only once when she had stayed late visiting in Owlswood. After that, she made sure she was safely back on her boat by 9:00pm.

The current population of owlpusses on Bong Tree Island number approximately 1,463. Most owlpusses live to be about 65 years old, although a few live longer, and the Owlpuss Oracle is said to be 137 years old, and the first owlitten of Barney and Caterina. Adults have no natural predators, plenty of food and water, and do not suffer from any ailments, so most die of old age and fly off to the Forever After Life where they happily watch over those they left behind on Bong Tree Island. The passing of an adult owlpuss is a natural event, and although the other owlpusses miss the departed one, they know he or she has gone on to an even more beautiful place.

In the past, hawks were known to take young owlittens or eggs, however owlpuss parents are fierce protectors of their nests and young, so it was a very rare occurrence. On the rare occasions when it had happened, the whole owlpuss community turned out to console the grieving and guilt-ridden parents and family.

The only way a hawk could take a young owlitten or egg was to wait until one parent had left the area to hunt or take care of other business, and then attack in a gang and overtake the remaining parent. There was no way a lone owlpuss could defend itself and its young against a gang of hawks, although they would fight valiantly, often to the death. If they survived, they suffered intense feelings of guilt and sorrow, which would take a long time to get over, although they eventually would, knowing that their young or unhatched had gone to the Forever After Life and were fine.

These days hawks have given up trying to steal owlittens and owlpuss eggs, after the owlpusses developed neighborhood watches so that no owlpuss is ever left alone on their nest without other family members or friends close by to help protect them.

"Male and Female Royal Doctor Hummingbunnybirds"

On all of Bong Tree Island, the Jeweled Doctor Hummingbunny-birds were the most adorable creatures Martine encountered. They are part hummingbird and part bunny. The males are very colorful and have two very long streamer tail feathers. The males also have the ability to change their color depending on the flowers they are feeding at, kind of like a chameleon. She saw them in green, red, orange, yellow, purple and even striped when feeding at striped flowers. When she asked why they did this, she was told that they changed colors just for the fun of it and because they could. This have no natural predators, so don't need to disguise or camouflage themselves for protection.

As with most birds, the females are drab colored and do not have the long streamer tail feathers. The Jeweled Doctor Humming-bunnybirds don't have beaks like normal hummingbirds, but instead have a long tubular tongue, which looks very much like a plastic drinking straw. They sip nectar with their tongue, but also nibble on clover, and zip back and forth all day long between Clover Meadow and the Multi-Colored Flower Field near Pigs Wallow. Hummingbunnybirds are very friendly and love to perch on your shoulder and wriggle their noses against your neck, which really tickles.

An interesting Bong Tree Island insect is the Fluorescent Blue Yellow Spotted and Fluorescent Green and Red Cat Paw Flutter-bydragonfly, which is a cross between a butterfly and a dragon-fly. It flutters around like a butterfly sipping nectar, but also has a set of dragonfly wings, which it can use instead to zip around when it wants to get somewhere fast. It feeds on both nectar and small insects.

The tail is actually a sewing needle, and in an emergency when an inhabitant of Bong Tree Island has been injured, the flutterbydragonfly arrives on the scene and sews up the wound with a thread that it secretes from its head, much the same way a silkworm creates silk.

The Fluorescent Blue and Green Flutterbydragonfly has been known to make overseas migrations of great distances, and were first discovered outside of the Bermuda Triangle in Gloucester, Massachusetts on Cape Ann by the renowned American team of Lepidopterists, Blythe Davis and Kim Smith.

And of course there are many bong trees, a very unique tree that only grows on Bong Tree Island.

CHAPTER IV

BONG TREES

"Bong Trees in Bong Tree Valley"

The bong tree (Sali arboret - meaning leaping tree) does not root in soil, taking its nourishment directly from the air, rain and sun, and leaps from one location to another at will, making a "bong" sound when it leaps. You can see a cluster of bong trees in one place and then see them in a totally different location a few minutes later. They occasionally move individually, but most often in a group, making a chorus of bonging sounds as they leap.

The owlpusses and birds on Bong Tree Island do not nest in bong trees because it is too easy for them to lose their nests. All bong trees look very similar so it is hard to tell one from another, and they can travel long distances. You do not want to seek shade under a bong tree on a hot sunny afternoon because just when you have gotten comfortable and started to doze off, it will leap away.

The bong tree bears a delicious, highly nutritious and satisfying fruit called a red, which looks like an orange, only it is red. It tastes like a cross between a honey banana and a strawberry and has the consistency of yogurt. The red has a thin outer shell which protects the fruit. You can crack the shell and use a piece of it like a spoon to eat the fruit. When the fruit is ripe, it separates from the tree but remains suspended in the air, which makes collecting them very convenient and easy, plus they never get bruised, broken or dirty from hitting the ground.

Although bong trees are located all over Bong Tree Island, the densest concentration of them is located in Bong Tree Valley, to the west of the Lioness Mountain Range. There you can see and hear the chorus of hundreds of bong trees, leaping from one part of the valley to another.

CHAPTER V

INTERVIEW WITH
SIR WINFRED OWLPUSS III

After Martine had freshened up and rested a bit, she went to conduct her first interview with Sir Winfred Owlpuss III, the owlpuss who greeted her when she arrived on Bong Tree Island.

Sir Winfred is a regal fellow, very outgoing and knowledgeable about the history and genealogy of the owlpuss clan. He told Martine that he is 87 years old and the sole surviving grandowlitten of "The Oracle", the first hatched of Barney and Caterina. Martine found Sir Winfred a pleasure to meet and interview. The only problem was that he kept offering her mice and seemed a little offended when she declined. She finally explained to him that humans don't eat mice; at which point he offered her a red instead, which she gratefully accepted and really enjoyed.

The owlpusses, or owlcats as some prefer to be called, love mice, which is the main staple of their diet. Sir Winfred told her that the younger ones had gotten ahold of, and really seemed to enjoy, Happy Puss cat food, but most of the older ones wouldn't touch it, because it does not contain any mouse.

Sir Winfred is the second oldest owlpuss on Bong Tree Island and acts as the spokesowlpuss for the others in disputes, generally involving something one of the ferrets or ferrowls had stolen.

Martine asked about the pea green boat filled with flowers on the shore of Crescent Moon Beach, and marveled at its impeccable condition. Sir Winfred explained that every year on the first day of the new year, the owlpusses celebrate "Year and a Day Day" to remember their ancestors, Barney and Caterina, and their journey which brought them to Bong Tree Island in 1871. The owlpusses have maintained the beautiful pea green boat Barney and Caterina traveled in, and on that day they fill the boat with flowers and dance around it.

Martine had arrived on an auspicious day, and he invited her to join them for the festivities after their interview. She thanked him and said she would love to attend. She then asked about other holidays that the owlpusses celebrated. He said that they did not celebrate any other holidays, but do remember everyone's hatchday and recite a poem to each owlpuss on their hatchday to honor them. The poem goes:

"On this day when you were hatched, the world became new. Your presence is unique and special, this fact is very true. We love you dear _____, life on Bong Tree Island would not be the same without you."

Sir Winfred was very knowledgeable on the genealogy of Barney and Caterina's progeny and history of events that had transpired on Bong Tree Island, and shared this information with Martine in great detail.

After they had finished the interview and painting session, Sir Winfred said it was time to go to the celebration. Since they had been meeting at Owlswood, near Crescent Moon Beach, he offered to walk with Martine rather than fly, so they would arrive together and he could introduce her to some of the others. It was taking a long time, since owlpusses can't walk very fast, so Martine asked if he would mind perching on her arm so they could move at a quicker pace and arrive in time for the celebration. Sir Winfred agreed and later said he really enjoyed the ride, and that it was his first time riding a human.

CHAPTER VI

YEAR AND A DAY DAY CELEBRATION

Martine and Sir Winfred arrived at Crescent Moon Beach a short time later to find the place packed with over a thousand owlpusses, as well as many of the other inhabitants of Bong Tree Island who turned out to take part in the festivities. The pea green swan-shaped boat was truly beautiful, especially overflowing with so many flowers. The dolphins were offshore in large numbers chattering away happily. The whales were singing so loudly that you could hear them from the shore.

Just then, everyone turned to look away from the shore and up into the sky. Martine turned and saw a parliament of owlpusses carrying what looked like a Venezuelan hammock woven from blood grass, with a magnificent owlpuss perched on it. Martine looked questioningly at Sir Winfred.

Sir Winfred explained that it was The Oracle, the oldest living owlpuss on Bong Tree Island and first hatched of Barney and Caterina, who was no longer able to fly the distance to Crescent Moon Beach from where she lived on Epiphany Peak in the Lioness Mountain Range. For the past seventeen years, a parliament of owlpusses had escorted her to the celebration. It was considered the greatest honor to be selected as one of the transport parliament for The Oracle, and all took their assignments very seriously. He confirmed that the hammock was indeed woven from blood grass by the resident flock of weaverbirds at Lionsgate, and explained that a new hammock was woven for her transport each year from a different grass or plant.

Sir Winfred said that The Oracle was incredibly wise and magnificent, and that he would arrange for Martine to have an audience with her soon.

Once the parliament of owls had reached the beach and carefully set The Oracle down in a place of honor where she could comfortably watch the festivities, the celebration commenced. The owls began performing the most beautiful dancing and singing while flying, swooping and diving over the beach and around the pea green boat. The other inhabitants joined in with their own variations of song and dance.

Sir Winfred introduced Martine to a turkey couple that was standing nearby, and excused himself to go find his wife and join in the celebration, telling her he would see her again soon.

Martine visited with the turkeys while continuing to watch the incredible display going on before her. The turkeys were an elegant couple named Tom and Henrietta, who lived on Turkey Hill and were descendants of the turkey, named Greer, who had performed the marriage ceremony for the owl and the pussycat in 1871. Henrietta said that Barney and Caterina's wedding had caused a great deal of excitement on Bong Tree Island, since no one there had ever seen an owl or a pussycat before, and in the short time between their arrival and marriage, they had become greatly loved by everyone.

Of course, not a single Bong Tree Island inhabitant saw the slightest thing wrong with an owl and a pussycat being married. Barney and Caterina had indeed chosen the perfect place to make their home.

Martine asked Tom and Henrietta if they would allow her to interview and paint them, at which time they could talk more about Turkey Hill and marriages on Bong Tree Island. They said they would be honored, and asked her to come by any time, but that if she wanted to witness a marriage, she could come on Weddingday afternoon at 3:00, when young owlpusses, Rick and Donna were to be wed.

Martine had had a long day, and was hungry and beginning to feel sleepy, so she excused herself and started to head to the clear stream to freshen up and pick some fruit before returning to her boat to go to sleep. She would have loved to just sleep in the soft aromatic grasses next to the river, but knew she probably wouldn't wake up in time not to get wet when the 4:00 am rains came.

Just then Sir Winfred flew over with two different looking young owlpusses in tow. He introduced them as the ferrowl brothers, Ferdi and Frankie, and said they were agreeable to being interviewed by her the next afternoon at 2:00.

He wished her a good night and said he would come by and call for her at 1:30 to show her where they lived. Martine said goodnight and thanked Sir Winfred for inviting her to the Year and a Day celebration, which she had enjoyed immensely.

CHAPTER VII

GENEALOGY OF
BARNEY AND CATERINA
AND CHRONICLE OF MAJOR
EVENTS ON BONG TREE ISLAND

• 1850, April 11, Barney and Caterina are born at the Bates Farm in Ramsgate, England.

• 1869, December 31, Barney and Caterina set sail from Ramsgate Harbor in the beautiful pea green boat.

• 1871, January 1, Barney and Caterina land on Bong Tree Island – they are both 21 years old.

• 1871, June 5 Barney and Caterina are married at Turkey Hill, at the age of 22.

• 1875, April 11, on their 25th birthdays, Barney and Caterina have their first kindlebrood of owlittens (4 of them). The Oracle (whose given name is Eve, which means life) was the first to hatch and is the only surviving owlitten of Barney and Caterina. She is 137 years old. The Oracle had 18 owlittens and 54 grand owlittens. Sir Winfred Owlpuss is her sole surviving grand owlitten. He hatched in 1925 and is now 87 years old and the second oldest owlpuss on Bong Tree Island.

• 1877, May 5, Barney and Caterina have their second kindle brood of owlittens (6 of them) – all are deceased. Between them they had 48 owlittens and 680 grandowlittens. 55 of their great and greatgreatgrandowlittens are still alive.

• 1879, November 11, Barney and Caterina have their third kindlebrood of owlittens (8 of them) – all are deceased. 73 of their great and great great grandowlittens are still alive.

• 1880, July 15, Barney and Caterina have their fourth kindle brood of owlittens (5 of them) – all are deceased. 67 of their great and great great grandowlittens are still alive.

• 1882, December 15, Barney and Caterina have their fifth kindlebrood of owlittens (7 of them) – all are deceased. 92 of their great and great great grandowlittens are still alive.

• 1885, December 11, Barney and Caterina have their sixth kindlebrood of owlittens (7 of them) – all are deceased. 153 of their great and great great grandowlittens are still alive.

• 1887, December 12, Barney and Caterina have their last kindle brood of owlitens (6 of them) – all are deceased. Owlivia is the last surviving grandowlitten from this kindlebrood. She was hatched in 1939, is now 73, the wife of Sir Winfred Owlpuss and the third oldest owlpuss on the island. Owlivia and Sir Winfred were married in 1964 had 6 kindlebroods of owlittens for a total of 42, all of whom are still alive and have given them 1,008 grandowlittens and 12 great grandowlittens.

• 1909, June 11 Alpheus Pomfry arrives on Bong Tree Island.

• 1909, September 16 the Mr. Pomfry Storm devastates Bong Tree Island.

• 1910 January-February, The Great Mouse Famine – thoussands of mice are stricken by the plague and 453 owlpusses die of starvation.

• 1914, November 18, Caterina dies at the age of 64.

• 1915, January 1, (on the 44th anniversary of Barney and Caterina's arrival on Bong Tree Island) Barney dies of a broken heart at the age of 64.

• 1916, January 1, The First Celebration of Year and a Day Day takes place, and has continued every year since.

• 2011, August 5, a cargo container filled with cans of Happy Puss cat food is discovered washed up on the shore at Crescent Moon Beach by a group of teenage owlpusses.

CHAPTER VIII

INTERVIEW WITH
THE FERROWL BROTHERS

Sir Winfred arrived at Martine's boat at exactly 1:30, which she found amazing, since owlpusses do not wear watches or have clocks, to take her to her appointment. Ferdi and Frankie, along with many of the owlpusses, live in Owlswood, not far from Crescent Moon Beach.

Owlswood is a beautiful wooded area of Bong Tree Island where Barney and Caterina made their home. Barney called it "Owlswood" because he was an owl, and mistakenly believed that his and Caterina's offspring would be owlets. He envisioned his progeny populating the area with owls, like himself. Imagine his surprise when Eve, their first hatched arrived on the scene and was an owlitten, with the body and claws of an owl, and the head and tail of a pussycat. Being a male, and a little too caught up in his owlness, he was taken aback at first, but quickly saw what a beautiful and unique creature his daughter was, and adored her to no end. Caterina on the other hand was wiser in such matters and not the least bit surprised.

These intense Happy Puss loving teen ferrowls are named Ferdi and Frankie. They told Martine how much they loved living on Bong Tree Island, but wished to travel one day and see other parts of the world. They asked many questions about the land beyond the line and were especially interested to know more about Happy Puss and where it came from. They also shared with her the story of how they had come to have Happy Puss cat food on Bong Tree Island.

One Frienday afternoon they and a group of their friends were sand bathing down at Crescent Moon Beach when they noticed a very large wooden container at the far end of the beach. They immediately flew over to investigate.

On the outside of the container was a picture of a can (although they didn't know what a can was) with an owlpuss face on it. They were very intrigued and excited to see their likeness and all started clawing at the crate until they were able to pull the boards apart, and out cascaded thousands of cans of Happy Puss cat food.

They bit and clawed at the cans, trying to figure out what they were. Then one owlpuss teen named Omar started pulling at the tab on the top of the can and the lid came off. Immediately the air filled with the most extraordinary aroma they had ever smelled. He tasted it and exclaimed, "This is the most delicious thing I have ever eaten – try it!"

They all took turns tasting and exclaiming about the wonderful treat that had washed up on their shore.

Because it was such an amazing treasure, they decided to hide the cans in a nearby cave so the ferrets wouldn't find them. They then each grabbed a can and flew home to show and share the incredible discovery with their families.

Needless to say, as in the case of Sir Winfred Owlpuss III, not all the adult owlpusses shared their excitement, being natural whole food enthusiasts, leery of the health benefits of fast food in a can coming from the land beyond the line. As it is with parents and teens everywhere, so it is on Bong Tree Island too.

Martine asked them how it was she hadn't noticed a single empty Happy Puss can around Bong Tree Island. They looked a little confused, and then Frankie said, "We love Bong Tree Island, this is our home. We would never leave empty cans around to mar its beauty or litter where we live. We carry the empty cans and stack them neatly in the back of the cave."

CHAPTER IX

INTERVIEW WITH OWLIVIA OWLPUSS

Martine's next interview was with Owlivia Owlpuss, lifetime mate of Sir Winfred Owlpuss III, and great grandaunt to Omar, Oswin and Otis, three of the teens who discovered the cans of Happy Puss cat food on the beach. Owlivia is old for an owlpuss, but still very spry and sharp, and at 73, she is a good deal younger than her husband. Unlike her husband, she was not totally against the can but thought it should only be eaten in small quantities as a treat and never allowed to replace the natural wholesomeness of mice, which contain all the vitamins, minerals and nutrients that an owlpuss needs.

She recalled a tale her great grandowlpuss The Oracle had told her when she was a young owlitten about The Great Mouse Famine of 1909. The mouse population had been stricken by a mysterious plague that killed thousands of them. As a result, hundreds of owlpusses starved to death. The tale had always made her a little fearful that such a devastating event could reoccur, and the stockpile of Happy Puss made her feel more secure. Though not the perfect food for an owlpuss, it could save many in the event of another famine.

While Martine's research has pretty well proved that Mr. Pomfry and his camera had nothing to do with the great storm of 1909, he may in fact have unwittingly been the cause of the Great Mouse Famine. Mr. Pomfry may have had stowaway mice on his boat, which made their way onto Bong Tree Island carrying some foreign disease with them, that then spread to the mouse population on the island. There is no other logical explanation for the plague and resulting famine.

Martine asked Owlivia how owlpusses view themselves as beings. Owlivia explained that the union of owl and pussycat had created a very unique and special being. Owls are the keepers of sacred knowledge and secrets of the Divine, and symbolize truth, wisdom, patience, clairvoyance and mysticism.

Cats encourage us to look within, and symbolizes creativity and psychic power, detachment, sensuality, desire, liberty, pleasure and magic. Owlivia also pointed out that owlpusses greet the world and everything in it through heart shaped faces, making love the natural state for them to project, and receive back in return. Put those characteristics together in one creature, and it is unique and special indeed, not to mention beautiful.

CHAPTER X

WEDDING ON TURKEY HILL

The next day was Weddingday, which Martine had been looking forward to. This was the day the owlpusses, Rick and Donna, were to be married at Turkey Hill, and she would get to experience a Bong Tree Island wedding ceremony.

She spent some time in the morning getting ready and then visited for a while with the hedgepiggywigs. At 2:00pm she headed for Turkey Hill. It was early, but she had not been there before and did not want to be late.

Turkey Hill is a lovely hill overlooking Crescent Moon Beach, and the perfect place for a wedding. Turkeys have lived here for as long as Bong Tree Island has been inhabited, and have been performing weddings almost as long. Turkeys are very serious, noble, and stately birds, so they are perfect for the job. They officiate marriages for all the inhabitants of Bong Tree Island, from mice to lions, hummingbunnybirds to owlpusses.

Before marrying, all couples are required to attend three premarital sessions with a pair of counselor turkeys, to make sure they are ready for marriage and understand everything they need to know to be good lifetime mates and parents. There have been some occasions when the turkeys have refused to marry a couple; generally because they are just too young and need a little more time to mature. The turkeys are very fair and impartial in their decisions, so no one gets upset if they are told to wait. All the parents on Bong Tree Island love the turkeys for this reason, in addition to the fact that they are generous, kind and very good neighbors.

For all the time that goes into the premarital preparation, the ceremony itself is very short, only lasting a couple of minutes. The vows went something like this:

"Do you Rick and Donna take each other to be your lifetime mates - to love, enjoy and protect each other, hunt together, share sunsets and sunrises together, care for and raise your young, and attend every Year and a Day Day celebration together until one of you goes to the Forever After Life?" They say, "We do", and the turkey pronounces them lifetime mates.

All the friends and family of the couple come to witness the vows and everyone cheers and flaps their wings (if they have them) when the turkeys pronounce them lifetime mates for the first time.

After the ceremony, Tom and Henrietta took Martine up to the bluff overlooking Crescent Moon Beach, which she thought was the perfect spot to do their painting.

CHAPTER XI

THE ORACLE

By far the most amazing owlpuss on Bong Tree Island is Eve, known as The Oracle. Martine journeyed to Epiphany Peak at the top of the Lioness Mountain Range in the central part of the island to have an audience with the Owlpuss Oracle. The Oracle, revered by all on the island, is the oldest and wisest of the owlpusses, and was truly a sight to behold. She is beautiful, with the countenance and glow of an angel. Her eyes are incredibly kind and deep, and it seems she peers straight into your soul and knows your deepest secret and greatest desire.

Martine spent a long time reasoning with The Oracle about the meaning of life, war and prejudice (which owlpusses know nothing of and were saddened to learn about), mankind's shortcomings as a species, and the Forever After Life. It was during their discussion about discrimination that The Oracle told Martine about the ferrowls.

A long time ago a young owlpuss named Pussandra met and fell in love with a handsome young ferret named Ferguson.

Now while ferrets are cheerful, playful and inquisitive, they are also opportunists, quick to take advantage and steal anything they can get their paws or jaws onto to be used at a later time.

Owlpusses on the other hand are wise, benevolent, kind, sweet dispositioned but serious, and do not understand thievery, as they know there is plenty of everything for everyone.

While owlpusses and ferrets lived in harmony as neighbors and accepted each other's differences, neither was ever considered a good match as a mate for the other. Before long young Pussandra found herself on the nest. Young Ferguson meanwhile was off having great adventures with his ferret friends.

Like all babies, Pussandra's were adorable; but they were not owlittens. Her young, which the others called ferrowls, were different. While they learned to fly and ate mice like owlittens, they also loved to play, hang out with ferrets, do weasel war dances (a very funny thing to see a ferrowl do), and get into things. They would also occasionally steal and hide items belonging to their mother, grandparents or neighbors.

Martine explained to The Oracle that in the land beyond the line, such a happening could unfortunately cause guilt and shame for Pussandra, Ferguson and their families, and ultimately result in the young ferrowls being discriminated against and treated differently, even badly. The Oracle found this news very sad. On Bong Tree Island, the ferrowls were accepted as a new species and enjoyed for their uniqueness. The owlpusses remember their ancestry, coming from an owl and a pussycat as they do. Barney and Caterina had been forced to leave their families and home in order to be together; and they would not wish anyone on Bong Tree Island to feel the need to do the same.

Martine then asked The Oracle how she had come to be so wise. The Oracle smiled and said she would share with her the secret to her wisdom. Most inhabitants of Bong Tree Island avoided the Bong Trees because their motion and speed made them uneasy, that and the fact that they don't talk and are viewed as standoffish and aloof.

As a young owlitten, Eve loved the Bong Trees and spent much of her time perched in them riding around the island. She enjoyed the thrill of the ride as they leaped, and the sound they made.

After a while she began to realize that the Bong Trees talked, but in quiet still voices that you had to be silent and listen for. They began telling her many amazing things that she had never heard before. Every day she would return to them and they would share more of their wisdom and knowledge with her.

The Oracle then told her that it was the Bong Trees who first introduced her to Epiphany Peak, a place they believe to be profoundly sacred, and where they go to seek enlightenment and to rejuvenate themselves. She is no longer able to go to Bong Tree Valley to visit them, but they come regularly to Epiphany Peak so they can visit and share new revelations with each other.

She has tried many times to explain to the others about the incredible gift of wisdom that the Bong Trees have to offer, but most continue to avoid them, being generally too busy chatting among themselves and making plans. One owlpuss couple, however had started spending time with the Bong Trees, so she is hopeful. She knows her trip to the Forever After Life could come any time, and she would love to know that another will follow in her footsteps as The Oracle.

At the end of their time together, Martine asked The Oracle if there was a message she would like her to take back and share with humankind. She stared into her eyes for a long time and then whispered, "My child, you know the message - all of creation knows the message. Treat others, as you would like to be treated yourself. Love and respect every living thing. Know that we are all one."

There was one last question Martine had to ask. "Dear Oracle, if we are all one and should love and respect everyone, then what about the mice?"

The Oracle smiled as someone smiles at a child asking a naive question, and answered gently, "We are owlpusses; mice are what we were designed to eat. We know that, the mice know that. Hummingbunnybirds were designed to eat nectar and clover. Sheep were designed to eat grass. We were designed to eat mice, and do not eat nectar or clover or grass, except on the rare occasion when we do eat grass to help rid ourselves of fur-eather balls.

We don't horde, never take more than we need, and we have the greatest love and respect for mice, as they are what sustain us. Mice also love and respect us and give themselves up to us in order to sustain themselves. They are very prolific breeders you know, and if we did not control their population, they would rapidly overtake the island, eat all the available food, and then starve to death. Did you know that the gestation period of a mouse is about three weeks, and that they give birth to litters of up to fourteen babies? One female can have as many as ten litters a year, and mice can have babies when they are as young as five weeks old, so the mouse population can increase very quickly if not controlled, and they know they can't control them-selves. We have a symbiotic relationship that serves us both well."

Just then two mice appeared and presented themselves to The Oracle and Martine. The Oracle bowed to the mouse, thanked him for his generosity, and then proceeded to eat him whole.

The other mouse stood patiently before Martine looking brave. Although she was feeling a little peckish, she told him that unless The Oracle was still hungry, he was free to go, as she did not partake of mice. The little one looked hopefully at The Oracle, who thanked him but said she was quite full. He went away with a look of disappointment on his face.

Apparently the mice draw straws each day to decide who will be The Oracle's daily meal, and it is actually considered quite an honor to be chosen. Most mice dream of one day being sustenance for The Oracle.

Suddenly a Bong Tree surrounded by ripe reds appeared, and Martine picked a few to eat during her journey back to Crescent Moon Beach.

Martine descended from Epiphany Peak filled with joy and optimism that, like the owlpusses and all those who lived on Bong Tree Island, maybe mankind also could one day live in peace and harmony – loving, respecting and sharing with each other.

CHAPTER XII

INTERVIEW WITH
OMAR, OSWIN AND OTIS

Martine's next encounter was with a set of triplet owlpuss teens named Omar (meaning first born son, as he was the first to hatch), Oswin (meaning a divine friend) and Otis (meaning keen of hearing, as he heard a passing hummingbunnybird upon hatching and looked up to see what it was). They are the great grand-nephews of Sir Winfred and Owlivia Owlpuss, and nephews of Grayson and Genevieve, who live near Pink Sand Beach on the north coast, close to Crystal Clear Lake.

Having grown up with their ferrowl friends, Ferdi and Frankie, they are much more playful and precocious than you would expect teenage owlpusses to be. They were there on the beach the day that the Happy Puss cat food was discovered and were the ones who suggested hiding the cans in the cave, knowing how the ferrets can be. Omar was the one who figured out how to open the can.

They said that they planned to fill the pea green boat with Happy Puss and sail away for a year and a day, as their ancestors had done. They would leave next year, the day after Year and a Day Day and be back in time for the following year's celebration, with great treasures and stories to share. Martine asked them what their parents and the others thought about their plan. They turned their heads in strange directions and looked sheepishly at her. Then Omar admitted that they hadn't talked about their plan with any of the adults, and guessed that they probably wouldn't think it was a very good idea.

Martine asked them if they remembered the story about the terrible Mr. Pomfry storm. They all said they knew the story well. Martine told them that Bong Tree Island was a very special place in many ways, but especially because of the weather, which was always so pleasant, and its beautiful calm Sea of Namaste. She explained that on the ocean outside the Bermuda Triangle, terrible storms with huge waves could come up without any warning and sink big ships, never mind what it could do to a little pea green boat, especially one filled with cans of Happy Puss cat food.

She explained that there were also pirates searching for boats to plunder, and huge tankers and transport ships that could run them down and sink them in a fog or dark night. Their ancestors had been very fortunate indeed to sail for a year and a day and make it safely to Bong Tree Island. She herself had just completed that journey and had experienced a number of harrowing events during the course of it, and her boat was much larger, had navigational aids on board, and she was a very experienced sailor.

She said that while their plan sounded like a great adventure, they would be taking their lives in their wings and should think long and hard about such a dangerous undertaking.

She told them that as far away as the line on the sea looks, it is further away than that, and that far again before you reach land. It is very easy to get lost on the ocean because you can't see land once you get out beyond the line, and how would they know which way to go. And think about how sad everyone would be if they couldn't find their way back and no one would ever see them or be able to celebrate Year and a Day Day or their hatch-days again. Martine reminded them that "life on Bong Tree Island would not be the same without you." They looked alarmed and agreed that they would consider what she had said and think about it some more.

CHAPTER XIII

GRAYSON AND GENEVIEVE

Martine's next interview was with Owlpuss couple Grayson (meaning son of the gray feathered one, whose father had gray feathers and fur) and Genevieve (meaning white wave), the aunt and uncle of Omar, Oswin and Otis and grandniece and nephew of Sir Winfred and Owlivia Owlpuss.

Unlike many of the other owlpusses on Bong Tree Island, Grayson and Genevieve had chosen to live in solitude near the Pink Sand Beach area of the island on the north coast, close to Crystal Clear Lake. It is an incredibly beautiful and peaceful section of the island, and Martine could understand why they had picked this area for their home. The mesmerizing Crystal Clear Lake is close by, with a pure and crystal clear source of water, and many mice live in the area.

The couple confided that they had chosen this place because of its peace and solitude. They had lived for a time at Owlswood, but the constant chattering of the dolphins, gobbling of the turkeys and talking of the other owlpusses was too distracting for them. They enjoyed spending time in the silence, and this was the perfect place for that.

They then started to say something about Bong Trees, but stopped. Martine immediately realized that they must be the couple The Oracle had referred to. Martine told them that during her recent audience with The Oracle, she had told her about the source of her wisdom, and about her life spent among the bong trees. The couple looked relieved and said that they had also been spending time with the bong trees, who were sharing much amazing knowledge and wisdom with them. They only wished they had listened to The Oracle years ago, but also understood that they had not been ready until now to hear and understand what the bong trees had to say.

As Martine was finishing up the painting of Grayson and

Genevieve, their precious and very energetic quadruplet grand nieces unexpectedly flew in for a visit. The energy of these four young teen owlpuss girls was intense, and they chatted excitedly and nonstop between themselves and at their grandaunt and uncle, all the while staring at Martine and giggling. When their excitement had settled a bit, Martine asked them if they would be willing to let her paint and interview them. That kickstarted their excitement to a new level, as they agreed in four animated high squeaky voices.

Since Martine had not yet been to Crystal Clear Lake, they decided to take a trip there for the interview and painting session. Grayson and Genevieve looked very grateful for the reprieve.

CHAPTER XIV

LIONESS MOUNTAINS
MANATURTLES
AND CRYSTAL CLEAR LAKE

Martine was very excited when the quadruplets suggested a trip to Crystal Clear Lake, as she had heard about it, but hadn't yet had a chance to see it. Crystal Clear Lake is a very large, very clear water lake near the Lioness Mountain Range, which you can see parts of mirrored in it.

The Lioness Mountain Range is where the lionesses spend most of the time raising their cubs, although it's name is due to the fact that the mountains look like lionesses, which is why the lionesses moved there in the first place. They do go to Lionsgate to spend time with the lions in certain seasons, but since the lions eat grass and don't need the lionesses to hunt and take care of them, the girls are free to spend their time together, which they prefer. Lions can be rather pompous and self-important.

The mountains have a number of deep caves, which give the appearance of lioness eyes from a distance. The quadruplets said that the caves are filled with bats, and another creature with red glowing eyes that no one knows much about because they don't leave the cave and no one has any good reason to go inside.

It is said that the lake is bottomless, and it has some very unique inhabitants. There is large lake monster, like a sea serpent or Bong Tree Island variety of the Loch Ness Monster that lives there, although Martine didn't get to see it. There are also lake manatees, turtles, many types of fish, including the multi-colored fluorescent glo fish that dwell in the bottomless part, and the rare painted manaturtles.

The painted manaturtles only exist in Crystal Clear Lake. It is believed that manatees traveled up the Three Rivers from the sea many years ago, found their way into Crystal Clear Lake and never left. They eventually became lifetime mates with the resident painted turtles, and their offspring became manaturtles. They are very curious and friendly, and will come to the surface to greet visitors to their home. They do not speak, at least not that Martine heard, but do make a soft humming noise, like a refrigerator but with a slightly higher pitch.

While they were at Crystal Clear Lake, a mother and baby manaturtle surfaced and visited with them a while, long enough for Martine to paint them. They love to eat young clover, but have difficulty getting it themselves, so Martine picked some that was growing nearby and fed it to them. While manaturtles will climb up on the rocks to bask in the morning sun, the clover patch is a little too far away for them to maneuver their cumbersome bodies to reach without great difficulty.

Manaturtles have very large, soft, hairy mouths with no teeth, a fact Martine came to know when they greedily sucked her hand into their mouths trying to get at the clover. When eating clover, the manaturtles smile and make a soft purring sound, like a contented kitten.

The quadruplets flew out over the middle of the lake, where the bottomless part is located, and called excitedly to Martine, telling her to swim out and see the fluorescent multi-colored glo fish. Martine considered it, as it was a beautiful day and the water looked luscious, but wasn't sure she wanted to chance running into the Crystal Clear Lake monster out there, so declined.

Although Martine is a brave explorer who has encountered many strange and often scary creatures and places during her explorations, she has made it a rule to avoid intentional encounters with sea monsters, anything with glowing eyes that lives in caves, and any place that includes the word "bottomless" as part of its description.

Later Martine ran into Hedgepiggywig Paul and asked him what he knew about the red-eyed creatures living in the Lioness Mountain caves. Paul said that they were Assiri, a type of aquatic cavedwelling fairy, and that their eyes were limpid blue, not red. They do carry red lanterns though, which from a distance are often mistaken for eyes. He said that they were very beautiful, enchanting creatures who would melt into a pool of water if touched by a ray of the sun. He said they loved moon-bathing, but were easily distracted and sometimes lost track of time.

It is said that Crystal Clear Lake was formed by melting Assiri who did not make it back to the caves in time before sunrise. They have been known to go out over the sea at night and lure men in ships with their beauty and red lights to crash into the reefs and rocky shores of Bong Tree Island. Many men who have disappeared in the Bermuda Triangle have been lured to a watery grave by Assiri. Crystal Clear Lake is a lake of karmic debt.

CHAPTER XV

PRECIOUS QUADRUPLETS

These precious quadruplet owlpusses, who just turned 13 this past weekend, are the daughters of Genevieve's niece, Matilda and her lifetime mate, Matlock. Their names are Clara (meaning bright), Naomi (meaning pleasant), Nora (meaning light) and Felicity (meaning happy).

Thirteen is the age when young owlpusses are first allowed to go off on Travelday or Frienday without their parents, as long as they have siblings or friends accompanying them. The girls had been on Travelday visits to Grayson and Genevieve's before with their parents, but not very often, so they were so excited to be traveling by themselves and able to do and go as they pleased without parents telling them it was time to go, or don't do that, or don't go over there. Of course they wouldn't do anything they had been taught not to do, even though their parents weren't there; but just knowing that if they wanted to, they could, and no one would stop them was very freeing and exciting. They had been planning this Travelday for months and were especially thrilled to have unexpectedly run into Martine and have their first human along on the trip with them.

The quadruplets chattered constantly amongst themselves, talking about this owlpuss boy or that one that they thought was really cute. All the while they were looking this way and that at things they had never seen before and pointing them out to each other.

They wanted Martine to tell them what young humans their age did in the land beyond the line. She explained that human girls did a lot of the same things as them. They talked about cute boys, they liked music and dancing, going to the beach, exploring and seeing new things, they liked shopping and malls, and they really liked being away from their parents and doing things with their friends.

Martine told them that some young human teens would not want to be seen with their parents and would pretend they didn't know who they were. The quadruplets thought that was funny and a little sad. They said they loved their parents, and although they were really enjoying being off on their own, they also liked going places and doing things with them too.

Then they wanted to know what shopping and malls were. Martine tried to explain, but the girls couldn't grasp the concept of either. The more Martine tried to explain it, the more confusing and foreign the concept became to her as well.

CHAPTER XVI

LIONSGATE

Since the quadruplets were out for their first adventure without their parents and were enjoying spending time with Martine, they asked her if she would like to visit Lionsgate. Martine excitedly jumped at the opportunity. She was sorry she wouldn't get to meet any of the lions, as they were still on retreat, but did want to at least see the place.

Lionsgate is a large area of rocks, moors and valleys with a beautiful view looking back toward Bong Tree Valley. It is where the lions and lambs spend most of their time, lying around eating grass. It is also the place where the wraiths wander in the pre-dawn hours.

The mysterious thing about Lionsgate is its entrance, and namesake. There are two large winged carved stone lions that flank the entrance to the region. These stone lions have been there as long as anyone can remember, and as long as history has been passed down. What makes them mysterious is that in all the history of Bong Tree Island, there have never been winged lions, nor does anyone have the foggiest idea how the statues got there.

There have been no known human inhabitants on Bong Tree Island (other than the wraiths, which are no longer really human) who could have carved them, and none of the inhabitants of Bong Tree Island own any tools or have the ability to accomplish that scale and level of craftsmanship with their beaks, teeth or claws.

It is one of those mysteries, like the ahu and moai on Easter Island, Stonehenge, or the Nazca Strip in Peru, which may only be explained by visitations in the past from extraterrestrial beings. Hedgepiggywig Paul did say that on occasion a large object with many lights has appeared at night and hovered over the island, especially near Lionsgate. After one such visitation, a

lion was reported to have gone missing.

It was starting to get late, and Martine had a long journey back, so said goodbye to the quadruplets and hurried back toward Crescent Moon Beach. She did not want to chance encountering the wraiths again.

The sun was starting to set as Martine reached the edge of the multicolored flower field. She realized she would not make it past Owlswood before dark and began feeling very uneasy. No one had given any indication that the wraiths were dangerous, but they really creeped her out.

Just then she heard a loud "bong" behind her and then felt a breeze rustle her hair as a bong tree flew past and stopped in mid air a short distance ahead of her. As she approached it, she heard a small quiet voice telling her not to be afraid and that there was nothing to fear except fear itself. The tree whispered that The Oracle had asked it to come and give her a ride home, and that if she so desired, she should climb up and hold on tight.

Martine felt an incredible sense of relief as she climbed onto the Bong Tree and held onto its branches for dear life. When a bong tree makes its leap, you want to make sure you are holding on very tightly, as it can propel itself from a standstill to 60 mph in 2.5 seconds.

They made it past Owlswood and on to Crescent Moon Beach in no time at all.

CHAPTER XVII

THE UNHAPPY BACHELOR

Martine's final interview was with a young bachelor owlpuss named Oscar, nicknamed Kip. Martine preferred Kip, so that is the name she used when talking to him. The only thing Kip wanted to talk about the fact that he was single and couldn't find a mate.

Kip was a little smaller than the other male owlpusses his age, but it was his stripes that were the cause of his problems. It seems that his stripes unnerved the female owlpusses because it made him look like a hawk, which made them instinctively distrust him. He was very concerned that he might go through life without marrying and having a mate and owlittens of his own. It made Kip feel especially bad because he was a very trustworthy owlpuss with lots of friends, who was very well liked by everyone, but none of the girls wanted to be his lifetime mate.

Martine asked him if he had ever considered another species for a mate, such as a ferret. Some of them have stripes, are a little smaller in size and are of a similar appearance to him, and there is precedent for such a union.

At that suggestion, Kip's face brightened and he grinned widely. In fact, there was one female ferret named Ferrina that was a good friend and always wanted to spend time with him. He really did like her a lot, but he had never thought of her in that way before.

Before departing Bong Tree Island, Hedgepiggywig Joey was announcing the exciting news that Kip and Ferrina the ferret were very much in love and had gotten engaged.

Martine predicts more ferrowls in the future of Bong Tree Island.

CHAPTER XVIII

THE JOURNEY
COMES TO AN END

As with all great adventures, the time for her stay on Bong Tree Island had come to its end. Martine was packing up her boat with fresh water, reds and other fruits, and coconuts. She had said her goodbyes to everyone, and was planning her departure for early the following morning.

Suddenly she heard a commotion on the beach and looked out to see a crowd of owlpusses and others from the island heading toward her. They had all turned out to throw her a farewell celebration and dance. They danced and sang until about 8:00pm then wished her a good night's rest and a safe voyage home.

As they were all leaving, she saw Omar, Oswin and Otis heading her way. They flew over and landed on the deck of the Good Morning Gloucester. She greeted them and asked how they were. They all said they were fine, and had come to ask her a special favor. Martine immediately thought they were going to ask to come with her, and didn't know how she would respond.

Omar, the oldest and the spokesowlpuss for the brothers, said: "We wanted to wish you a safe journey, especially after all you told us about the dangers out on the ocean. We also wanted to say that we hope you come back to visit us one day, and if you do come back, do you think you could bring us some more Happy Puss?"

Martine breathed a sigh of relief, laughed and promised the owlpuss brothers that if she returned, she would certainly bring them more Happy Puss, and some other special treats.

She was sorry she hadn't gotten to meet the lions and lambs at Lionsgate or the Assiri at Lioness Mountain Range (now that she knew they were fairies and didn't have red glowing eyes,

she wanted to meet them), and there were a few other regions and inhabitants of the island she had not gotten to explore and meet.

The next morning she set sail at 6:00 am. As she was leaving Delphinidae Bay, a large pod of dolphins swam in front of her boat chattering and laughing. She realized they had come to lead her out of the Bermuda Triangle. She was very grateful, as she did not know how she was going to find her way out, since compasses and other navigational equipment do not work in the Bermuda Triangle. She was really enjoying the sail -- the weather and wind were perfect and the dolphins cavorting ahead of her made her smile and feel very peaceful and content.

As they approached the exit to the Bermuda Triangle, the dolphins' behavior suddenly changed. Their playful chatter turned to warning cries, and they all started looking off to starboard. Martine felt a sudden chill and was overcome with a feeling of dread. She followed their gaze and saw off in the distance a large dark schooner with blood red sails that was just entering the Bermuda Triangle.

The ship had a familiar ominous look and feel about it. She grabbed her binoculars to get a closer look, and was alarmed to see that it was a pirate ship with a number of evil looking hands on deck, plus two large vicious dogs, and a number of huge rabid looking ship rats. She quickly recognized it as the pirate ship that had pursued her during her journey to Bong Tree Island, which would have overtaken and captured her had that pod of whales not intervened and stopped them in their tracks so that she could escape.

Martine immediately became concerned that the pirates might find their way to Bong Tree Island. Fortunately no dolphins were making a move to lead it.

She suddenly felt someone watching her and looked up into the crow's nest to see a dreadful scarfaced pirate looking at her through his spyglass. Cold chills ran down her back and she gasped in fear that they might again attempt to give chase and capture her.

Suddenly she crossed over the line of the Bermuda Triangle, and the dolphins and ominous ship disappeared from sight.

Martine breathed a sign of relief, charted her course and set sail for England.

One interesting fact that should be pointed out here is that it only takes 30 days to sail from England to the Bermuda Triangle. It takes another eleven months and a day from the time you enter the Bermuda Triangle to reach Bong Tree Island; however it only feels like a day. It is a strange time warp phenomenon that only exists in the Bermuda Triangle. Of course, it was Hedge-piggywig Paul who explained this phenomenon to Martine.

Upon her arrival back in London, the Queen greeted Martine with much pomp and circumstance and threw a lavish party in her honor at Buckingham Palace. She spent two weeks with the Queen, telling her all about the trip, sharing the interviews and paintings she had done of the descendants of Barney and Caterina, as well as other inhabitants of Bong Tree Island, and telling her the sad news about Mr. Pomfry.

Martine had brought back some reds to share, which the Queen dearly loved and wished there were more of. Although she had packed many of them for the return trip, she had eaten most of them herself during the voyage.